I2461160

Tales from Shakespeare

Romeo and Juliet

Lord and Lady Montague
Romeo's parents

Friar Laurence
A Franciscan monk and
Romeo's confidant

Balthasar
Romeo's servant

Nurse
Juliet's adored and
trusted servant

Paris
A nobleman who wants
to marry Juliet

Lord and Lady Capulet
Juliet's parents

Benvolio
Romeo's cousin
and friend

Mercutio
Romeo's friend

Romeo
The Montagues' son

Juliet
The Capulets'
daughter

Tybalt
Juliet's cousin and
heir to the Capulet
fortune

Prince Escalus
The prince of Verona
and local leader

C. A. Plaisted

Illustrated by Yaniv Shimony

QED Publishing

Families at war

Act one

In the streets of Verona, a fight had broken out between servants of the Capulet and Montague families. Before long, some of the young men of the families had joined in. Even Lord and Lady Montague had arrived to exchange insults with Lord and Lady Capulet.

In fair Verona, where we lay our scene

"I've had enough of all of you!"
said Escalus, the prince of Verona. "The
Montagues and the Capulets have been
feuding for years. This has got to stop! Go
home. If you don't keep the peace,
I will punish you all!"

The Montagues and
the Capulets
did as they
were told. No
one wanted to
get on the
wrong side
of such an
important man.

Lord Montague
had asked his nephew, Benvolio, to look
out for his son. "He seems so sad these days,"
Montague had said. So, on his way back to
the Montague house, Benvolio went to look
for his cousin Romeo.

What sadness lengthens Romeo's hours?
– Benvolio

Benvolio soon found his cousin moping in the street.

"What's wrong, Romeo?" Benvolio asked.

"Oh, I am lovesick for beautiful Rosaline!" Romeo said.

"And there I was thinking something was wrong," laughed Benvolio.

"It is," wailed Romeo. "Rosaline has no idea how I feel about her. And I have no chance of meeting her."

"Well, we'd better find a way of making it happen," Benvolio consoled him. "Come on – let's get back to the house!"

The cousins hadn't gone far before they were stopped by a servant.

"Excuse me, sirs," the servant said, scratching his head. "Can you help? I don't know who the people on this list are..."

"Let me see," said Romeo.

He read aloud the names of all the important people of Verona. All the Capulet family were included, but none of the Montagues.

"It's an impressive list. And I see Rosaline is on it," Romeo said. "Why do you need to know who these people are?"

"They're invited to the Capulet house for a masked ball," the servant said. "I thank you, sir, for helping me. Why - you should come too! You're not Montagues after all..."

As the servant rushed off, Romeo turned to Benvolio.

"A masked ball with Rosaline there. And now we've been invited..."

"Let's go," Benvolio said. "With a disguise, no one will know who we are. Let's hurry and find ourselves some masks."

Inside the Capulet house, Lord Capulet was talking to a young nobleman called Paris. Paris had been admiring Capulet's daughter, Juliet, for a long time.

"I'd like to marry Juliet," Paris declared. "And soon."

"I can't deny you'd make a great husband for her," Capulet said. "But Juliet's so young!"

"Plenty of girls are married at her age," Paris argued.

"True," agreed Capulet. "But take things slowly, Paris. Make sure you win Juliet's heart."

Paris nodded.

"Come on." Lord Capulet put his arm around Paris, chuckling. "Let's go down to the party."

Upstairs, Juliet was getting ready for the ball with the help of her nurse when her mother came in.

"Juliet," her mother said, taking her hand. "In just two weeks you will be fourteen — the same age I was when I had you. Your father has told me some exciting news about Paris..."

Juliet blushed. She knew Paris was a handsome man, but he was a lot older than her.

"He wants to marry you!" Lady Capulet declared.

"What a catch he'd be for Juliet!" Juliet's nurse exclaimed.

Juliet blushed deeper.

"I haven't even thought about getting married," Juliet said.

"Well, go off to the party and think about it!" Lady Capulet said.

Her daughter nodded.

Romeo, Benvolio and their friend Mercutio met outside the Capulet house, disguised in their masks. In the moonlight, the house twinkled with party decorations. Surely no one would realize they were Montagues?

But as they got to the door, Romeo felt nervous. What if his enemies spotted him?

"I don't think this is a good idea," Romeo said. "We should go..."

"No, gentle Romeo," Mercutio said to his friend. "This is your chance to meet Rosaline!"

> If love be rough with you, be rough with love
> – Mercutio

So, with their masks on, the three friends entered the ball.

Inside, the Capulets' guests were enjoying the party of the year. Lord Capulet was pleased to see everyone dancing and having fun.

Meanwhile, Romeo was searching for Rosaline. He saw a girl by the window. She'd taken off her mask. Romeo's heart fluttered.

"Who is that?" he wondered aloud. "I have never seen anyone so beautiful."

O, she doth teach the torches to burn bright!

– Romeo

Tybalt, Juliet's cousin, was standing nearby. He'd heard what Romeo had said.

"That voice..." Tybalt hissed. "It's Romeo Montague!"

Tybalt rushed to tell his uncle.

"Don't worry," Lord Capulet told him. "I've heard young Romeo is a good boy. He won't cause trouble, and nor should you. Just ignore Romeo for tonight."

Tybalt backed away, angry that his uncle wouldn't stand up to Romeo.

Romeo had no idea he had been recognized. All he could think about was the girl at the window. Romeo walked over to her and took her hand.

"You are the loveliest girl I have ever seen," whispered Romeo, taking her hand. "May I steal a kiss?"

Juliet blushed. "I shouldn't..."

Romeo leant towards her and their lips touched. Juliet's face flushed.

"Who are you?" Juliet asked.

But before Romeo could answer, Juliet's nurse arrived.

"Your mother wants to speak to you," she said, sending Juliet away.

You kiss by th'book
– Juliet

Romeo's eyes followed her as she walked away. He turned to the nurse.

"Who is her mother?"

"She's Lady Capulet, of course," the nurse replied. "And Juliet is too good for you! Now go. Don't cause trouble here."

Romeo left the ball, his heart beating heavily. How could the most beautiful girl he had ever seen be a Capulet?

Star-crossed lovers

Act two

Back in the Capulet house, Juliet ordered her nurse to find out who her sweetheart was.

"Who was that boy? I hope he isn't already married – go and find out!"

So Juliet's nurse sneaked out of the house to catch up with the handsome boy.

She returned with shocking news.

"His name is Romeo. He is the son of Lord Montague!" her nurse exclaimed.

> My only love sprung from my only hate!
> – Juliet

"Come now. He's gone. Let's get up to your room..."

Distraught to hear that Romeo was her enemy, Juliet followed.

Meanwhile, in the Capulets' garden, Benvolio and Mercutio found Romeo still thinking about Juliet.

"Forget about her!" said Mercutio.

"Come on," Benvolio agreed. "Let's go home."

"No," Romeo said. "Leave me."

So Romeo's friends left. Alone in the garden, Romeo could not stop thinking about Juliet. How would he ever be able to see her again?

Just then, Romeo saw a light coming from a balcony.

Oh Romeo, Romeo, wherefore art thou Romeo?
– Juliet

"Oh, it is my love!" he said. "I wish she knew I was here."

Sheltered by the trees, Romeo stood quietly. He had eyes only for Juliet.

"Oh, Romeo!" Juliet said as she looked out into the night. "How I wish you were not a Montague. But it's just a name... Names mean nothing!"

Romeo crept towards the Capulet House. He climbed up the vines to Juliet's balcony. "Sweet Juliet," he whispered once their eyes met, "I would gladly change my name for you!"

Under the cover of night, the pair talked for hours. Neither of them had ever felt love like this before.

"Marry me, Juliet," Romeo begged. "We can tell our families afterwards. We can make them see that we no longer need to be enemies!"

"Oh Romeo – I will!" sighed Juliet sealing her promise with a kiss. "But you must go," Juliet warned as the sun began to rise.

Parting is such
sweet sorrow
– *Juliet*

"I will miss you every minute I am not with you."

"Then I will return as soon as I can," Romeo said.

"Goodbye for now," said Juliet as Romeo left.

He ran off, keen to arrange their wedding.

Romeo knew just the man to speak to: Friar Laurence, a priest he trusted to keep his secrets. It was now early morning, and Romeo found the friar in his garden. Excited with the first flash of love, Romeo told him his news.

"But what happened to Rosaline?" the puzzled friar asked.

"I've forgotten all about her," Romeo explained. "I have met the love of my life – Juliet Capulet!"

For this alliance may
so happy prove, to
turn your households'
rancour to pure love
  – *Friar Laurence*

The friar thought for a while. Perhaps this love between the children of enemy families might solve their quarrels at long last.

"Bring Juliet here this afternoon," the friar agreed. "If marriage is what you want, I will help."

Back at the Montague house, Mercutio and Benvolio realized that Romeo had not come home from the ball.

"Don't look so worried, my friends," Romeo announced when he finally appeared. "All is well."

But Romeo kept the news of his wedding to himself. In fact, the only person he told was Juliet's nurse, so that she could pass on the details to his love.

Alone in her room, Juliet was fretting. Her nurse had left over an hour earlier to find Romeo and hear his news. Now Juliet was worried Romeo had changed his mind.

"Everything is fine," Juliet's nurse reassured her when she returned. "But be quick! You must race to Friar Laurence. That's where you will find Romeo, waiting to make you his wife."

Juliet ran as fast as she could to Friar Laurence's chapel.

Romeo gasped when he saw her. She was even more beautiful than he remembered.

"Oh, Juliet!" he said, taking her hand. "Can I possibly make you as happy as I am?"

Juliet nodded. "If you marry me, yes."

So smile the heavens upon this holy act, that after-hours with sorrow chide us not
– Friar Laurence

"Well, let's not waste any more time then," said Friar Laurence. "Come inside and let me make you husband and wife."

Just a few minutes later, Juliet Capulet became a Montague.

Tempers and temperatures soar

Act three

It was hot and steamy that day in Verona. Tybalt and his friends were angry. How dare those Montagues enter the Capulet house last night! They were prowling the streets, looking for trouble, when they spotted their enemies nearby.

"Well, look who it is!" sneered Mercutio. He had been cooling off with Benvolio under the trees, but now leapt to his feet. "Can we help?"

"I want a word with you!" Tybalt spat.

"Gentlemen, gentlemen," said Benvolio, pulling Mercutio back. "We don't want any trouble. Come on, Mercutio, we should go."

And if we meet
we shall not scape
a brawl
– Benvolio

But Tybalt and Mercutio couldn't resist the opportunity for a fight. They both drew their swords and waited to see who would pounce first.

"No!" cried a voice from behind them. It was Romeo, fresh from his wedding and still starry-eyed with love. "Let's not fight on this beautiful day," Romeo said. "You dare to say that to me?" Tybalt replied. "You, who snuck into my home and insulted my family?"

"I meant no harm," Romeo protested. "Why, I think of your family as my own."

But poor Romeo was the only one that knew of his link to the Capulets.

"Leave him alone!" shouted Mercutio, pointing his sword at Tybalt.

Clack! Tybalt smashed his own sword down on Mercutio's. With one mighty lunge, the sword pierced Mercutio's side.

Blood oozing from his wound, Mercutio staggered away.

"Get me help!" he gasped. "You are villains for doing this to me. I curse both your families!"

"What have you done?" Romeo screamed as Tybalt and his friends fled.

A plague o' both your houses!
I am sped!
- Mercutio

On the pavement, Benvolio held Mercutio in his arms.

"Oh, Romeo!" he wept. "He's dead!"

"What started as the best day
of my life has now become the worst,"
Romeo said as he stood weeping beside his
dead friend's body.

Just then, a snigger came from around
the corner. It was Tybalt and his friends.

"He's standing there gloating at what
he has done!" exclaimed Romeo, wiping tears
from his eyes.

And without a moment's thought,
Romeo leapt to his feet and
went after Tybalt.

"All of this is your
fault!" Tybalt declared,
pointing his sword at him.

"I don't care if it is!"
screamed Romeo.

> Thou wretched boy,
> that didst consort
> him here, shalt with
> him hence
> - Mercutio

And with one mighty thrust of
Romeo's sword, Tybalt fell down dead.

"You've killed him!" Benvolio yelled.
"Quick – you must go! The prince will
punish you for this!"

O, I am fortune's
fool!
– Romeo

Romeo stood frozen on the
spot. He'd not only killed a man,
he'd killed his wife's cousin. She
would never forgive him.

"I am such an idiot," Romeo cried.

Suddenly, he heard voices. People were
coming out of their houses to see what was
going on.

"Why are you still here?" Benvolio
hissed. "Go! Now!"

Without another word, Romeo
ran away.

The street was now full of people.
Even the prince appeared when he heard
there had been yet another fight between
the Capulets and Montagues.

"What has happened here?" the
prince bellowed.

"Tybalt killed Mercutio," Benvolio
explained. "And now Romeo has taken
revenge and murdered Tybalt!"

"This madness must stop," said the prince. "I am banishing Romeo from Verona! He must never come back!"

Back in the Capulet house that night, Juliet was alone in her room, waiting patiently for Romeo to return.

"We're ruined! Everything is ruined!" wailed Juliet's nurse as she burst into the room.

"What are you talking about, nurse?" Juliet asked.

Between fits of weeping and sobbing, the nurse told Juliet of the morning's terrible events.

O God! Did Romeo's hand shed Tybalt's blood?
- Juliet

"Romeo killed Tybalt?" Juliet asked in disbelief. "My darling Romeo has been banished?"

"How can you talk like that about the man who killed your cousin?" the nurse sobbed.

"How can I speak badly of my husband?" Juliet said. "A husband I will never see again..."

Seeing Juliet's torment, her nurse felt sorry for her.

"Stay here," she said. "I heard Romeo is hiding with Friar Laurence. Perhaps I can sneak him in here to see you."

O find him! And bid him come to take his last farewell!
– Juliet

Hiding with Friar Laurence, Romeo was in despair. And when the nurse arrived to tell him of Juliet's own agony, he felt even worse.

"I might as well have killed Juliet herself," Romeo wailed.

"Stop," Friar Laurence said. "This isn't the answer. Juliet needs you now more than ever. You must go to her."

"I want that more than anything," Romeo agreed.

"But afterwards you must leave," Friar Laurence warned as Juliet's nurse nodded. "Go to Mantua. Put some distance between yourself and these terrible events."

"I will tell Juliet," Juliet's nurse said, and rushed back to the Capulet house.

"And I will follow you in secret," Romeo said, shaking the friar's hand.

Lord and Lady Capulet assumed that Juliet's tears were in mourning for Tybalt.

"We need some happiness in this house," Lord Capulet declared as he sat talking with his wife and Paris, late that night. "Something to look forward to."

These times of woe
afford no times
to woo
— Paris

"Do you think, perhaps, you might let me marry Juliet now?" Paris asked. Lord Capulet looked at his friend.

"Wife," Lord Capulet said, "Go and remind Juliet how much Paris loves her. Tell her they shall be married this week!"

"Husband," Lady Capulet said, smiling. "I will tell her first thing tomorrow. This is very good news indeed!"

The Capulets had no idea that their daughter was already married, and even less that her husband was their enemy, Romeo. Or that at that very moment, he was entering Juliet's bedroom...

Early the next morning, Romeo and Juliet awoke to the singing of a lark.

Wilt thou be gone?
It is not yet near
day. It was the
nightingale, and not
the lark.
          – Juliet

"You're not going already, are you?" Juliet said. "It's not yet daylight."

Romeo took his wife's hand. "If I stay, I will be killed," he said, solemnly. "But if I go, it will be as if I'm already dead. I can't live without you."

They both knew that there was no alternative. Romeo had to flee Verona.

"Will we ever see each other again?" Juliet asked.

"We will," Romeo replied. "I promise."

The star-crossed lovers kissed goodbye.

"I pray that he returns to me," Juliet said as Romeo crept out of the Capulets' garden and went to meet Friar Laurence.

All around Verona, people were
waking up to a new day. In the Capulet
household, Lady Capulet called her
daughter to see her. She told Juliet that
she would marry Paris that
same week.

"Marry Paris?" exclaimed
Juliet. "I can't! I won't!"

"Stop being ridiculous," Lady
Capulet declared. "He's a good
match for you."

"But I don't love
him!" Juliet cried.

Their shouting brought
Juliet's father and her nurse to
see what was going on.

"Don't be so disobedient!"
Lord Capulet said. "If
you don't marry Paris, I will
never speak to you again."

"Help me!" Juliet wailed
to her mother.

32

But Lady Capulet agreed with her husband. "Don't expect sympathy from me, young lady. I've had enough of your nonsense!"

Left alone with her nurse, Juliet wept.

"Perhaps, you should marry Paris," said the nurse. "He's handsome – and he's rich!"

"But I already have a husband," Juliet sobbed.

She thought for a while. What could she do? Perhaps Friar Laurence would have the answer.

"I am going to take confession with the Friar," Juliet told her nurse and, with a heavy heart, she left.

Friar Laurence comes up with a plan

Act four

"Hello, wife!"
Juliet approached the friar's front door. Could that be Romeo calling her, she wondered? But no, it was Paris standing at the friar's door.

"I cannot tell you how happy I am," Paris said, kissing Juliet's hand.

"Sir, forgive me," Juliet whispered, lowering her head. "I am here to take my confession."

"Of course," Paris said, nodding. "I will say goodbye – until our wedding day."

"Oh friar," Juliet wept as Paris left. "You must help me get out of this engagement. I would rather kill myself than marry Paris!"

"No, no!" the friar shook his head. "There's no need for that. I have a plan. One that means you and Romeo can be together."

"Tell me," Juliet pleaded.

"First, go home and tell your parents that you will marry Paris," the friar said. "Then, the night before the wedding, you must take this potion."

The friar handed Juliet a small bottle.

"Drink this and you will fall into a deep sleep," the friar continued. "So deep, everyone will think you have died. Then you will be brought to this tomb."

Juliet stared at the friar.

"Instead of having your wedding, your family will be preparing for your funeral," he explained.

"And I will write to Romeo in Mantua, telling him to come and take you away from here forever!"

Juliet hugged the friar.

"Give me the potion," she said. "My love for Romeo will let me carry out your plan."

The Capulets were delighted when Juliet told them that she would marry Paris. The wedding invitations were sent out immediately.

Love give me strength, and strength shall help afford
- *Juliet*

Juliet felt cruel deceiving
her parents, but she knew that
it was the only way she would see
Romeo again.

That night, alone and
frightened in her room, Juliet
drank the potion that the
friar had given her. Within
minutes, she fell into a sleep
so deep she seemed dead.

The next morning, when it was
time to wake the bride, Juliet's nurse
gasped when she found Juliet lying still
on her bed.

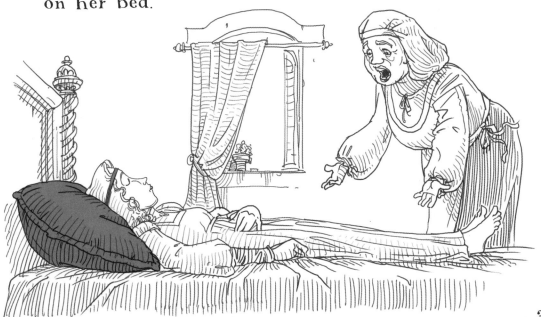

"My Lord! My Lady!"
Juliet's nurse shrieked. The
Capulets rushed to their
daughter's room.

"She's dead!" Lord
Capulet wailed.

"It can't be true,"
Lady Capulet wept.

"There will be no wedding music here
today," Lord Capulet said solemnly as
Juliet's body was taken away. "Instead,
we will be singing sombre hymns."

Two young lovers meet their fate

Act five

As Juliet's body lay in the Capulet vault in Verona, in Mantua Romeo was unaware of the friar's plan.

I dreamt my lady came and found me dead
– *Romeo*

Romeo's servant, Balthasar, had raced to Mantua to find his master as soon as he heard the news. He arrived before the friar's letter.

"I am so sorry to bring you this terrible news," Balthasar said, telling Romeo of his wife's death.

Romeo was distraught. How could this have happened?

How could his happiness have been taken away from him again? If he couldn't be with Juliet, he didn't want to live at all.

After telling Balthasar to leave him, Romeo made his way to an apothecary and bought a bottle of poison. The apothecary assured him the poison was so strong that it could kill him in an instant.

Back in Verona, Friar Laurence was waiting for Romeo and preparing to wake Juliet from her sleep.

But instead of Romeo, the man who had been sent to deliver the letter to Romeo appeared at the Friar's door.

"Isn't Romeo with you?" Friar Laurence asked.

The messenger shook his head. "I never made it to Mantua," he explained. "I was held up in Verona."

"Then I must hurry and send another letter to Romeo," Friar Laurence exclaimed. "Juliet will be awake within three hours – I must rush!"

But Romeo was no longer in Mantua. He was already racing back to Verona, overcome with grief at the news Juliet was dead. He planned to drink the poison as he lay with Juliet in her tomb.

The Capulets' terrible misfortunes had cloaked Verona in sadness.

Paris had gone to sit outside the Capulet vault, praying for Juliet. He was kneeling there when he heard Romeo approaching.

"It's that murderer, Romeo!" Paris hissed, drawing his sword to attack. "Stop, you vile Montague!"

He lunged at Romeo, who was quick to fight back. Romeo stabbed Paris.

"You have killed me," gasped Paris. "Bury me with my Juliet."

Romeo leapt back. Could it be true? Had he killed again? Romeo watched as Paris dropped to the ground.

Horrified, he turned
to the Capulet vault. Inside,
he found his beloved Juliet
laying peacefully in her
death-like sleep.

Romeo gazed at his
wife and placed her hand
in his.

"Oh, Juliet! You are so
beautiful. Let me kiss
you one last time."

Taking the bottle of poison
from his pocket, Romeo drank
it all and collapsed on
the floor.

Moments later, Friar Laurence returned to the vault.

"What's this?" the friar gasped. He found Paris dead outside and Romeo's body lying on the floor inside.

"This cannot be true... Paris is murdered and Romeo looks so pale... No! He's dead too!"

"Friar? Is that you? Where is my Romeo?"

The friar turned to see Juliet waking from her sleeping potion. He frantically tried to shield her from the devastation.

"You must leave!" he pleaded and rushed off to get help.

Seeing her dead husband
slumped on the floor,
Juliet ignored
the friar.
"My Romeo!
What is this in your
hand? Poison? Is it still
on your lips?" Juliet kissed
him. "Your lips are still warm, my love..."
She could hear voices outside the vault.
"I must be quick!" Juliet cried,
grabbing Romeo's dagger. "I will die by
my husband's side."
Piercing her heart with the dagger,
Juliet collapsed beside Romeo's body.

A short while later, the friar returned to the Capulet vault. He brought with him the prince and Lord and Lady Capulet. As they took in the terrible sight, Lord Montague arrived.

Montague hung his head in sorrow at the terrible scene that lay before him. "This is too much to bear. My wife also died tonight, overcome by grief at Romeo's crime and punishment."

The Prince asked for the vault to be sealed up. He then turned to the friar.

Friar Laurence lowered his head, wishing that he had never been part of this terrible tragedy. He told the prince and the bereft parents how the young couple had fallen in love, but were cursed by their feuding families.

How they had secretly married, but Juliet had been ordered to marry Paris. How his letter has gone undelivered and ultimately led to so many tragic deaths.

The prince turned to the Capulets and Lord Montague. "Your children falling in love could have been your chance to make peace," he said. "Instead, you have punished everyone."

Lord Capulet and Lord Montague promised that from that very day the feud would end – forever. They shook hands and wept.

For never was a story of more woe than this of Juliet and her Romeo

The End

Consultant: Dr Tamsin Theresa Badcoe
Editor: Alexandra Koken
Designer: Andrew Crowson

Copyright © QED Publishing 2012

First published in the UK in 2012 by
QED Publishing
A Quarto Group company
230 City Road
London EC1V 2TT

www.qed-publishing.co.uk

All rights reserved. No part of this publication may be reproduced,
stored in a retrieval system, or transmitted in any form or by any
means, electronic, mechanical, photocopying, recording, or otherwise,
without the prior permission of the publisher, nor be otherwise
circulated in any form of binding or cover other than that in which
it is published and without a similar condition being imposed on the
subsequent purchaser.

A catalogue record for this book is available from the British Library.

ISBN 978 1 84835 831 7

Printed in China